Disclaimer

This is a work of fiction. Names, characters, organizations, spots, occasions and occurrences are either the results of the creator's creative energy or utilized as a part of an invented way. Any similarity to real people, living or dead, or genuine occasions is absolutely adventitious.

ISBN:1946792195
 eBook: 978-1-946792-03-7
print:978-1-946792-04-4
audio/d: 978-1-946792-05-1

© **2017 Urquhart Randolph**

Published by Glofton llc

Table Of Contents

VISIT US

WWW.GLOFTON.COM
Enroll in our VIP list.
Be the first to be notified on our latest published book.
Downloading for free, free gifts.

THE SEARCH FOR ONENESS

CHAPTER 1

Vanessa McFall, a seventeen-year-old, is the last child and only daughter of her parents. Her Dad is Mr. Stevie McFall – a business Tycoon, Eva McFall – her belated mom, and Nicholas McFall – her nineteen-year-old big brother. They live in Dallas, Texas. Two years ago, when Vanessa and her brother were 17 and 15years respectively, Eva died in a fatal car crash.

Some local folks believed their dad was behind her death whiles others believed Vera, who was then their father's secretary and alleged secret lover, was solely responsible for her death.

On the contrary, police investigations and reports suggested that it was purely an accidental plight. Just a year later, he married his secretary, Vera, who is fifteen years younger than him and just eight years older than Nicholas, his son.

Newly wedded Mrs. Vera McFall, moved into their mansion in Dallas after their honeymoon but endured a strained relationship with Vanessa and Nicholas McFall because of the rumors they had heard.

Vanessa trusts her father knew nothing about it, that Vera carried out the execution by herself and is in for her dad's money whereas Nicholas believes that the act was contorted by a collaborated effort of the duo. After just a week of their marriage, Vanessa gave her father a three-day ultimatum to break the collapse it because she couldn't stand seeing Vera in the house.

He failed to comply with the ultimatum because he loved Vera too much let go but this got Vanessa heartbroken. She felt her dad had chosen Vera over her and since then, she became cold-hearted towards her dad. Nicholas, not making things any better, swore that they would never earn his respect for as long as they remained married and he became an absolute family rebel ever since.

As the months passed by, the chemistry within the McFall family grew weaker and weaker but it didn't stop Stevie McFall from organizing a one-year anniversary ceremony of his marriage to Vera. He threw a very big banquet, which had many

Dignitaries and people of the highest status quo attend it. However, Nicholas and Vanessa didn't hesitate to crush the soiree.

Although there was no physical violence whatsoever, things got really awry and nasty when Vanessa took the mic and addressed the audience – branding her stepmom as the lady she believes to have caused her mom's tragic death.

There was shock amongst the guests, rumors and whispers circulated throughout the crowd and it was just impossible for Vera to stay at the party without crying. She fled the scene, weeping uncontrollably and her husband followed to console her. In the end, they had to drive away just midway through the occasion.

After the incident, for a week, Stevie went into serious thinking, hoping to find a way to settle his kids' minds on the issue. After serious deep thoughts and analysis, he comes to believe that the local folks are responsible for his kids' numerous evil misconceptions and the only way to curtail that would be to relocate.

A few weeks later, he bought another mansion in Princeton, New Jersey. He had decided to leave the management of his investment company in the hands of Kieran McFall, his junior brother and business associate, with the hope of gradually establishing another branch in Princeton and occasionally checking up on the one at Dallas.

He informed his wife and kids about the decision and told them they would leave in two weeks' time, when Vanessa and Nicholas have vacated. The kids were repulsive to the news but he maintained his stance and they were to leave on August 1 1998.

CHAPTER 2

It's August 1 1998. The McFalls arrive in Princeton and Stevie drives them to the new house. It's a beautiful mansion, more glorious and bigger than the one in Dallas. Stevie expects them to be as elated as Vera is but the kids are rather sorely displeased at the sight of it. They are pissed because Vera, their dad's new undeserving money hungry wife, is about to live with them in a mansion more glorious than what their mom has ever had.

Mr. McFall opens the door to the house, holds Vera's hand and makes her the first to enter. She hurries into it and is amazed by what she sees.

She turns around excitedly and hugs the person behind her, thinking it's Mr. McFall but as she does, she notices it's Nicholas and withdraws swiftly.

He looks at her distastefully and, knowing exactly what that look means, she attempts to apologize but he raises his right hand towards her, slowly molds a fist and then let the middle finger out to signify *"fuck you."*

Vera's ecstatic mood drops instantly but Vanessa bursts out into a seemingly unending irritating round of laughter and walks past her. Vera is saddened for a moment but doesn't make it get the better of her. She quickly joins up with her husband who is just outside and chatting with one of the drivers. Mr. McFall enters later with his wife and shows everyone to their room. He proposes to show them around the house but the obstinate kids refuse.

Later in the day, Stevie tells his wife that he'd forgotten to do a very important thing which he must return to Dallas to complete but will be back in two days. Vera prepares supper in the stead of the cook who will arrive the following day and calls everyone to come eat but the other two, just as has become of them in the past year, refuse to sit at table with them. They prefer eating in their bedrooms.

Later in the night, Mr. McFall goes into Vanessa's room and informs her he has to leave the next morning. However, she tells him she's not interested in whatever he's doing and doesn't really care. He's hurt but unable to do anything to change his daughter's feelings. He goes into Nicholas' room to deliver the same info but the response is not any better from his end. The night passes quietly and very early on Monday morning, Mr. McFall leaves for Dallas.

Vera knocks on Vanessa's door at 8am. Vanessa allows her in because she thinks it's her dad at the door but upon seeing Vera, she yells, 'What the fuck do you want in my room?' Vera tries telling her breakfast is ready but she wouldn't even listen. She yells, 'Get the fuck out of my room!'

Vera, fed up and pissed by Vanessa's standoffish attitude, says to her, 'Look, I don't argue with kids ok. You can go suit yourself.' She turns about and slams the door.

Nicholas, who is next door, virtually hears everything. He hurries towards his door and locks it. Vera hears the sound of Nicholas' key lock and she knows what to expect – she doesn't even bother to knock on his door. She retreats downstairs and takes breakfast alone at the dining.

At 9am, Vera meets all the workers at the hall to brief everyone on their responsibilities and her expectations. While the meeting is ongoing, Nicholas descends from his room upstairs, walks in, and –ignoring everyone – switches on the TV. He increases the volume to its maximum and then gets out of the house to take a stroll on the street. Vera ignores him and puts the TV off.

Fifteen minutes later, Vanessa descends from her room and walks into the hall while Vera is still in the meeting.

She walks straight towards Vera and asks rudely, 'Where the hell is my fuckin bro?' Vera ignores her and carries on with the interview. Vanessa walks behind her and screams into her left ear, 'Where the hell is my fuckin bro, bitch?'

Vera loses her temper. She stands up instantly and slaps her. Vanessa holds her cheek in anguish and bursts into tears instantly. Upon seeing the tears drizzle down her cheeks, Vera feels remorseful suddenly and regrets what she'd just done. She gets out of the sofa and hurries towards her to apologize but Vanessa runs outside immediately and takes to the street.

Nicholas finds himself a basketball court about 500 meters away from the house. He joins the dudes, exhibits his unrivalled basketball playing skills and they are all enthralled by his display. He introduces himself and some of the girls get their heads turned after hearing he's a member of the wealthy family that had just moved in.

He takes particular interest in one girl who is more reserved, Yvonne, when he requests to speak with her, she smiles and declines from speaking with him. He gets to chat with almost all the girls and Emily, the hottest among them, leaves with him.

By the same time, Vanessa has been sitting on the shores of Lake Carnegie. She is sad and mad at herself for being so soft and not hitting Vera back.

After sitting there for over an hour, she notices a guy seated about thirty meters to her left. He's been sitting there for as long as she could remember. She stares at him for a while and tries to figure out what he might me doing. She's caught off-guard on one occasion as he turns his head to his right and catches her staring at him. He waves at her before she realizes the person she's been staring at has noticed her too. She waves back briefly and looks away.

Moments later, someone taps on her shoulders. She looks over her shoulders and finds a young handsome and muscular guy standing behind her. He smiles at her and she smiles back. He sits by her and engages her in a very entertaining chat with her. He offers her a bottle of wine to drink. From the corner of her eye, she sees the other guy at the far left signaling to her not to drink it but she ignores him. In a matter of a few minutes, she begins to feel very drowsy.

The big guy stands her up, supporting her waist with his hands, and begins to walk her away but she's too drowsy to ask why or where he is taking her. Even though she would like to scream. Her vision worsens from blurry to dark and then she falls unconscious.

Nicholas arrives home at 12pm with Emily and sees Vera seated at the hall. Emily says hello to her but Nicholas ignores her completely.

Just as they begin to climb upwards, Vera hurries towards him and enquires worriedly from Nicholas if he has seen his little sister but as usual, he does the "fuck you" sign to her face. They get into the room and Emily asks him who Vera is and why he treated her like that. He tells her not to bother because Vera is just a whore who has come to spend his dad's money.

Nicholas enters the bathroom to wash down and upon his return, he sees Emily's clothing and underwear scattered on the floor and her body buried beneath the bedcovers. His dick leaps for joy. He drops his towel instantly and joins her in the bed.

Vera is worried that at 1:30pm, Vanessa isn't back yet. She decides to enquire from Nicholas again. As she draws closer to Nicholas' door to knock, she hears Emily moaning so loudly out of ecstasy – Her hand is stayed on the door instantly, unable to knock. She leaves, returns an hour later and knocks.

Emily opens the door and walks past her but Nicholas refuses to get out of the bed. She walks in and informs him that Vanessa had not returned but he doesn't pay the least attention to her and that gets Vera frustrated. She gets into the street and begins her personal search for Vanessa.

CHAPTER 3

Vanessa regains consciousness and finds herself lying on a bed in a cabin. She's so scared and tries to recall what had happened earlier. Although feeling a little frail, she gets out of the bed and walks towards the door. She hears someone's footsteps approaching as she nears it.

She quickly picks a besom lying on the floor and leans stealthily against the wall close to the door. The door opens and just as the person walks in, she strikes the head with the besom before realizing it is a harmless young girl.

She shouts, 'Ouch!' and drops the pizza in her hand. Vanessa looks on, terrified and regretfully as she tends the injured part of her head. The lady looks at Vanessa and says to her somberly, 'I mean you no harm.'

Vanessa is still confused and dumbstruck. She watches on as the lady picks up the box of pizza from the floor and makes her way to the bed. She puts the pizza on the bed and asks Vanessa to come sit by her. Vanessa takes a seat and apologizes to her.

She asks the lady how she got there and what she was doing there. She tells Vanessa her name is Yvonne and that her brother rescued her from the clutches of a rascal. She tells her he is making barbecue outside and that she could ask him what had happened.

They finish the pizza; Yvonne takes Vanessa to her brother and she leaves the two alone to chat. He smiles at Vanessa but she struggles to smile back.

She takes a moment to recall where she'd seen that face before and she finally remembers that that was the guy sitting at the shores of the lake. She's finally able to smile back and says, 'You were the guy at the lake, right?'

He smiles again and says, 'I think there were two guys.'

'Oh yea, but I mean you're the one that waved at me. Right?'

'Okay, now you're being more specific.'

'Can you please tell me what happened? How did I get here?'

'Oh, you don't remember? The guy you fell for drugged you.'

'O my God. I remember I was feeling drowsy and he picked me up. But no, I didn't fall for him. After seeing what my brother does with ladies, I don't trust men. I was just happy because I was sad and he was making me happy.'

'Okay, if you say so.'

'But please, did he do something to me? What did he do to me?'

'He did nothing.'

'No please, don't lie to me. How did I get here? What did he want with me?'

'Alright, alright, I'll tell you. He was going to put you in his car, take you to his home – wherever that is – and rape you, maybe use you as a sex slave or maybe worse; kill you.'

'Oh my God!' She screams, 'I never knew such stuffs were real. He looked so innocent and charming.'

'Well, what's most important is you got lucky.'

She asks doubtfully, 'But how could you have rescued me? He looked so tough.'

'I actually saw him when he came. He was the only one who'd come with a car and when I realized you were beginning to feel drowsy, I knew my fears were right. I ran to his vehicle and punctured all the tires.'

'That's it?' She asked curiously.

'Yes. He definitely thought that probably someone had seen him, suspects him and has sabotaged him. The best thing for him to do by then was to leave you alone and run, and maybe return later for his car.'

'Wow. I would never have thought like that.' She says wryly.

She accepts a piece of meat from his barbecue and eats it before realizing she'd not even asked of his name. He tells her his name is Peter and an eighteen-year old. At 5pm, Yvonne wakes up from her rest and sees them having a nice time together. She joins in the conversation and gets to know Vanessa is new in the neighbourhood and is the junior sister of the boy she'd met earlier in the day.

They walk Vanessa home and they arrive at the front of the mansion at exactly 6pm. She asks them to come along but they decline to.

Meanwhile, Vera has been sitting worriedly and scared with the security man at the security post for about an hour. Upon seeing Vanessa at the gate, she jumps to her feet excitedly, runs towards her, lifts her up with a hug and says with teary eyes, 'Vanessa, I'm so sorry. I promise I'll never ever hit you again. I'm so sorry. I was so worried and scared.'

Vanessa tries to play nice with her because she knows Peter and Yvonne are watching. – After how nice they'd been to her, she wouldn't want them to think she's a rude person. She waves them bye and walks with Vera across the compound and back into the house. Immediately they get in, Vanessa draws herself away from her stepmother rudely, runs into her room and locks herself up.

As she lays in bed, she ponders over everything that had happened during the day. She believes, for the first time ever, that she was touched by Vera's tears. However, her mind is predominantly occupied by memories of the moments she'd spent alone with Peter. She smiles to herself as she ponders how handsome, gentle and kind he was.

At 9pm, Vera knocks on her door and requests that she allowed her apologize but she wouldn't let her in.

She writes a note of apology and pushes it beneath the door. Vanessa reads it and her heart is touched by the words but her mind isn't willing to love nor forgive her.

Meanwhile, after having roved through town and checked out every corner where pretty young girls could be found, Nicholas returns home at 10pm and again, he is with Emily. They enter his room, lays her down, strips off her clothing and fucks her.

She's so loud that Vanessa can hear her from her room and that irritates her. She picks a pillow and moves downstairs to sleep at the hall.

THE UGLIER RIDE

CHAPTER 4

It's 9am in the morning the following day. Everyone is already up and has taken in breakfast prepared by the chef

Vera puts in frantic efforts to get Vanessa and her brother to come down and meet the workers for official introduction but only one does – Vanessa.

They introduce themselves to her as; Jim – the 26year old chef, Juan – the 24year old maid, Anita – maid and 18year old sister of Juan, and Joe – the 40year old gardener.

Nicholas descends and sees them introducing themselves but he ignores them, walks out and heads into the street for another busy day.

Vanessa shakes hands with them and hurries out, making her way for the main gate. Vera pursues her, halts her at the gate and asks her where she is headed. She takes offence to the question and replies with a cheeky answer. Vera apologizes and explains to her that she needed to know for her own safety, and also to answer her dad if he called. In order to haste away, she tells her she's headed for the lake.

Stevie calls shortly afterwards on the telephone. He informs her he wouldn't be returning that day but rather on the weekend. Vera virtually weeps on the phone, reminding him it's impossible dealing with both kids alone but he assures her everything will be fine and that the weekend is just at the corner.

Vanessa reaches Peter and Yvonne's cabin but it's empty. She recalls Peter had told her he usually spends time at the lake during the early hours of the day while Yvonne loves to watch the local boys play basketball. She goes to the lake and meets Peter sitting around the same spot he was a day ago. She sits by him and they begin to have a lengthy interesting conversation.

Meanwhile, Nicholas is at the basketball court displaying his unique talents once more and wowing the crowd.

He notices the girl that had caught her attention the previous day – Yvonne – is present and that spurs him on to do more showboating to impress her. He sees her clapping and shouting to cheer some of the moves he pulls off and he figures that means she is already so impressed. After the training ends, almost every girl tries chatting with Nicholas but Yvonne begins to walk away. He cuts short the conversations and runs after her.

He tells her he likes her attitude and personality and would like to be friends with her. She admits that she admires his skills but not interested in his friendship. Nicholas insists and persuades her but she maintains her stance and walks away without giving out her name nor address. Emily catches up with him and they head for the house.

Yvonne reaches the cabin and sees Peter searching through her belongings while Vanessa is seated on her bed. Peter halts and tells her Vanessa has been insisting she wants him to give her swimming lessons and that he was searching for one of her unused swimsuits. Vanessa bends and pulls a large paper box from beneath her bed.

She pulls out three new swimsuits and tells Vanessa to make a choice. She chooses a beautiful purple swimsuit, Peter walks out and she dons the costume which looks great on her.

She accepts a big blue towel from Yvonne and they join Peter outside.

Peter and Vanessa make their way to the lake, which is just about a five minutes' walk away from the cabin but they are not joined by Yvonne who explains to them that she has to go see a friend.

Vanessa had had a couple of swimming lessons in the past but she quitted because she was never really interested but this sudden interest of hers is so because she wants to have fun with Peter. Peter gives Vanessa her first ever swimming lesson in a lake. She is so elated during the session and on their return, she climbs onto his back, telling him she's too tired to walk.

Meanwhile, at home, Nicholas takes Emily through a very hot fucking session after which she washes down, dresses up and lies beside Nicholas. She asks him if she could consider him her boyfriend and whether he loved her. Contrary to her expectations, he tells her she's just a sex mate to him and that he's not that weak to fall in love after a mere sexual intercourse. Emily is grossly disappointed, heartbroken, and with tears in her eyes she sets off.

As she passes by Vera who is seated at the hall and discussing with the chef what to cook for supper, Vera notices Emily is leaving with teary eyes. She shortens her talk with the chef, climbs upstairs to Nicholas' room and enters through the door which is lying ajar.

Upon seeing her, Nicholas turns his face towards the wall. Nevertheless, she sits on the bed and speaks to him.

'Nick, I know you hate me but don't do this. Stop hurting innocent girls. Women are not toys to be played with.'

He turns around, chuckles and says to her, 'But my old bald dad plays with your young firm tits, right?'

'Please! At least, show me some level of respect.' She rebuts.

'Respect? Respect!' Nicholas retorts, 'respect is what you need? Okay, fine.'

He springs out of the bed, hurries to the door, locks it and begins to take off his shirt. Vera stands up from the bed instantly, retreats into the corners of the wall and says in a jittery tone, 'Nick! What are you trying to do?'

He chuckles and says whiles taking off his shorts, 'Well, as far as I'm concerned, you're not my mom and you're not my dad's wife.'

Vera sinks into the corner of the wall and pleads tearfully, 'No! Please Nick, you can't do this' but he doesn't bulge. She wrestles him but he's too strong for her. He overpowers her, carries her off the floor, throws her unto the bed, rends her blouse, skirt and bra. She screams but she's not heard from the other parts of the house because it's too big. She holds her breasts firm with her hands but that enables him to finally rend her panty too.

He forces his knees between her thighs to get them wide open and pins her hands tightly to the mattress. She sees Nicholas' huge erect dick staring her right in the face but she is almost out of energy to fight back. She shuts her tear-drenched eyes and stops fighting back. Nicholas, thinking the time is right, attempts to guide his dick into her pussy with his left hand but this releases her right hand which she spontaneously whacks wickedly into his testicles.

Not knowing where Nicholas had thrown the keys, she runs into his bathroom and locks herself inside whiles he rolls on the floor in agony. The pain subsides and after about an hour, he picks himself up and walks towards the bath door.

He stands behind it and cries hypocritically, asking Vera to forgive him but she says nothing. He pleads with her to, at least, not tell his dad but she still says nothing. He dresses up, and tells her he's leaving the house so she can finally come out of the bathroom. He unlocks the door and walks out.

Vanessa who has just returned from a nice time with Peter meets Nicholas at the gate who walks past her hurriedly. She's not alarmed because she knows her brother is guilty of having mood swings.

She makes her way across the compound, into the house, and towards her room. As she gets to her doorstep, she realizes Nicholas' door has been left partially open which seldom happens.

She decides to have a peep in. When she does, she sees a lady come out of his bathroom in a towel. She withdraws her head and then peeps again to see who it is. She notices it's her stepmom and her heartbeat begins racing. She sees Vera picking her clothing and undergarments from Nicholas' messy bed.

Before Vera makes it out of Nick's room, Vanessa tiptoes quickly away from the door, through the hallway and speeds downwards to the hall. She sits at the hall, flabbergasted by what she had just seen.

CHAPTER 5

Three days pass and on the Saturday morning, Stevie McFall returns from Dallas. He is met by Vera at the airport and they come home.

In the past few days, Vera has not been herself because of the ugly experience she had suffered but, Upon Stevie's return she puts on a pretence as though all is well. She drives him home and they arrive there at 11am.

He announces his presence enthusiastically but Vanessa, who's seated at the hall, isn't the least moved by it. She's filled with so much disdain upon seeing his dad enter in with his hands around Vera's waist but is unable to let it out. Stevie notices her indifference, walks towards her and sits beside her in the couch.

He kisses her forehead; assures her he loves her and asks if everything is okay. She is so enraged and wants to let the cat out of the bag but she still holds her piece. She merely nods to her dad.

He enquires of Nicholas from Juan who joins them at the hall and is told he's gone out. Juan takes Stevie's travel bags upstairs to the master bedroom while he sits with his wife at the hall in the presence of Vanessa but Vanessa is filled with so much disdain when Stevie gets Vera onto his laps that she could virtually feel the rage boiling in her chest. She gets out of the hall and climbs up into her room because she can't bear the sight of her dad cuddling and sweet-talking Vera but Vera herself is not in her usual ecstatic mood.

After lunch, Stevie decides to take Vera to the beach and proposes that Vanessa joined them but she refuses. They leave at 1pm and Nicholas shows up few minutes later. He makes his way through the hallway, enters his room and locks the door.

Anita who has been assigned to cleaning and maintaining Nicholas' and her sister's room has not been able to touch Nicholas' room in the past three days due to his unstable movements and strict routine of always locking his door. Now that he has arrived, she picks up her cleaning equipment and hurries upstairs. She knocks on his door and identifies herself.

Nicholas lets her in, closes the door and locks it. She is a little concerned that Nicholas had to lock the door but she keeps her fear concealed. Nicholas helps with her bucket, holds her by the waist and takes her further into his room.

'So you clean during afternoon's too?' He says gently while sitting her on the bed.

'Umm... it's usually in the mornings but sometimes you are either not here when I knock or you may be sleeping.'

'O, okay. So I'm a nuisance to you then, I guess.'

'Oh no, no that. It's my job so I have to make sure I get it done. No matter what it takes.'

'Okay, so where are you gonna start from?'

'Umm… the bathhouse.' She says, pointing her hand in its direction.

Nicholas holds her nervous shaky hands, stares right into her eyes and asks, 'Are you scared of me? Why are you so jittery?'

She looks away shyly and says, 'No, I'm sorry. I'm just a nervous girl.'

'So how long will this cleanup last then?'

'Maybe an hour or two.'

'Do you mind if I helped you?' he says with a cute smile.

With an innocent look on her face, she says 'Oh please, no. Thanks but I have to do this by myself.'

Nicholas agrees and allows her to start the cleanup. He stands at the bath's entrance while she does and engages her in a humorous conversation. She's almost done with the bathroom after about 20minutes and Nicholas is already drooling over sexing her. He walks closer while she is finishing up with the bathtub and opens the shower on her.

She's startled and jumps out from beneath it. Nicholas mocks her playfully and she's stuck between pissed and excited. She resumes and Nicholas does it again. She flees from beneath the shower and gets out of the bathtub.

'What are you doing?' She asks, feeling ambivalent at the time – wishing to play and yet fearing to do so.

Nicholas ignores the question and tickles her. She laughs. He does it again and again until she's fully caught up in a strong ambience of joy. Nicholas stops for a moment and looks her in the eye but she looks away shyly. She notices her blouse is wet, embarrassingly exposing the trace of her bra. She turns around ashamedly to hide it from him. He takes a step closer, hugs her from behind and wraps his hands around her waist. Her heart thumps suddenly.

He says to her, 'It's okay dear, don't be scared' but she frees herself from him and steps into the bathtub to pick the sponge and brush. Nicholas follows her in and holds her again; his hands wrapped around his waist from her behind and his chin resting gently on her shoulders.

He kisses her pinna and that sends a strange sexual sensation through her. She attempts to free herself but his grip is a little tighter. She kisses it again and again, then kisses her neck lustfully. She begins to moan pleasurably. He switches on the shower and their clothes are totally drenched in water within a few seconds.

He gets his hand into her wet skirt and then panty – she really wishes to stop him but it's already too pleasant for her. As he touches her clits and begins to rub them gently, she loses it and begins to moan more intensely. He puts off the shower, walks her out of the tub and removes her wet clothing. She's left with just her panty and bra which she refuses to let him take off.

He carries her into his bed, squeezes her breasts and sucks seductively on her belly button. He manages to pull her nipples out of her bra and begins sucking on them too. She becomes so engulfed in pleasure and just when he puts her hand into her panty, she halts him again. He looks at her and she has a bittersweet look on her innocent face.

'What is wrong? You're not enjoying it?' He asks.

'I am' she says shyly in a sober tone, 'but I've never done this before. I'm a virgin.' He looks at her for a while, smiles and just when she loses a little concentration of the hand in her panty, Nick rubs his thumbs over her clits and she begins to lose herself.

He tells her to close her eyes and she does. He slips her panty sideways and sticks his penis into her tight wet pussy. She opens her mouth widely, as if to gasp for air, and moans very loudly, pulling and clinging onto the beddings.

Vanessa who is already pissed at his brother and stepmom but has been unable to confront either of them can hear them from her room. She gets even more annoyed and frustrated. She gets out of her bed, brushes her hair, walks out of the house and heads towards Peter's place. She arrives there at 3pm and sees Yvonne chatting with a male friend whiles Peter is in his swimming costume, about to go swimming.

She enters Yvonne's room, picks up the swimsuit Yvonne had gifted her and joins him. They spend another nice time together. Peter tells her the guy she'd seen with Yvonne is her lover.

She asks Peter about his and he says he has none. He tells her everything about himself and their parents who are deceased and she tells him about hers too but declines to talk about her recent headache – her brother and stepmother's sexual escapade.

They return to the cabin at a quarter past 5pm and meet Yvonne and Matthew – her fiancé – who announce to them that they will be leaving town the next morning with Matthew's family for a week to spend the holidays.

Meanwhile, Yvonne has already packed her stuff and will be spending that night with Matthew's family. Vanessa and Peter change into their regular clothing, accompany them to pick a cab, and then Peter sees Vanessa off at her gate.

Vanessa waves him and enters the house. Just as she reaches the hallway to their bedrooms, she sees Anita coming out of Nicholas' room. Anita is startled upon seeing her and the look on her face, coupled with her messed up hair is very suggestive to Vanessa that she's been fucked. Anita greets hair guiltily and shamefacedly but Vanessa walks past her and into her room without saying a word.

CHAPTER 6

It's 7pm same day and the couple are not back yet but Vanessa is lying on her bed and reading a romance novel. There's a knock on her door and she asks whomever it is to come in.

The person enters and walks towards her but she doesn't take her eyes off the pages till she stops beside her bed. She looks up and it is Anita. Vanessa had begun to like Anita and been nice to her but after what she'd seen this day, she has no more admiration for her.

Yet, she chooses not to exhibit her disgust towards her. She tells Vanessa her parents had just called and they said they would be spending the night at the hotel.

She's already so furious upon hearing the news that her dad will be spending the night at a hotel with that shameless adulterous stepmom of hers but right after Anita leaves her room, Vanessa hears a knock on Nicholas' door and she knows it's Anita. She hopes she's just there to deliver her information. When Nicholas shuts his door and locks it, she's not sure whether Anita is there with him or not but she decides to mind her own business. After some minutes, she begins to hear Anita's voice penetrating through the walls to her room – Nicholas is fucking her and she is moaning irrepressibly.

Vanessa thinks she's had just about enough of everything – her stepmom probably fucking her dad already after fucking her brother, and her brother fucking her favorite maid irritatingly to her hearing. She gets out of her bed – so mad at herself – and sets off to Peter's place.

Peter is surprised to see her at that time but welcomes her. He asks her why she'd to leave the house and come over by that time. She tells him she's just bored because there is no one to talk to and her parents were not spending the night at home. At 10pm, he tells her it's very late and that she has to leave but she refuses. She pleads strongly with him to let her spend the night there.

They chat and watch TV until 12pm when she doses off. Peter carries her to Yvonne's bedroom and lays her on the bed.

Vanessa wakes up the next morning around 6am. She rinses, walks out of the bedroom and finds Peter in his swimwear, getting ready to leave. She remembers he had told her he likes to swim best when it's very early in the morning; the water cool and fewer people around. She puts on hers too and follows after him. They spend almost two hours swimming and by the time they return, it's 8am. Vanessa enters Yvonne's bathhouse to wash down with soap whiles Peter does same in his own bathroom.

She stays under the shower for some minutes before putting it off, and then she pours shampoo into her hair. Just when she needs the shower again and opens it, it just won't flow. Some shampoo gets into her eyes but there's no water available to rinse it. She stays her position helplessly, eyes shut, and unable to open them but as it gets more and more painful, she begins to cry out Peter's name.

Peter, half naked with just a small towel covering the lower part of his body, runs to her aid and stumbles on her nakedness. He looks confused but she pleads with him to run and fetch her some water. He runs to his bathroom and returns with a bucket of water.

He hands her a towel to wrap herself in and he helps throw water into her eyes to rinse the shampoo off. She submerges her head in the bucket of water to rinse off the remaining shampoo in her hair and then Peter helps her get to the bed.

She sits on the bed looking embarrassed and her eyes reddish. Peter is guilt-ridden for having chanced upon her nudity. He turns around to walk away because he's already having an embarrassing erection that has puffed up the towel and is so obvious.

He enters his room and obliviously leaves the door ajar. He lies backward on his bed, slots his right hand into his towel and begins to fondle his hard erect dick – daydreaming what a sexual moment with her would be.

Vanessa enters his room two minutes later with just a panty and a bra beneath the towel she has on and is utterly shocked upon seeing him in the act. 'What are you doing?' she asks surprised. Peter realizes her presence, shuts his legs immediately and sits up with an embarrassing look on his face. She sits by him on his bed and there's absolute silence for almost a minute until Vanessa speaks.

'It's okay if you want to fuck me.' She says bluntly and shyly.

'No, Vanessa… I'm really sorry about…' She shushes him in the middle of his statement.

'Last night, I wanted you to but I couldn't say it. Now, I realize you would like to and I'm cool with it. After all, someone gets to fuck someone eventually and life goes on.'

'Vanessa, I've really dreamt of having sex with you' he admits shamelessly, 'but it's not like I just want that. I need more than just sex.'

'What do you need, then? Money?'

'Definitely no! It's you I need. I love you.'

'You want me to believe your love for me is the only thing driving you to wanna fuck me? Come on, I know that kind of talk. Just fuck me. I'm not gonna bear a grudge against you if you don't love me.'

He holds her hand and looks into her eyes, 'I love you Vanessa. Do you love me too?' She's short of words at the moment but acts impassively although she's feeling a strong deep amorous emotion. She gets up from the bed, refusing to answer the question, and returns to Yvonne's room where she dresses up and leaves.

WHEN MESSIER GETS MESSIEST

CHAPTER 7

Vanessa reaches home at 9am in the morning and just about when she's entering her room, Nicholas is coming out of his. He says hello to her but she ignores him rudely and walks into her room. Nicholas doesn't understand why she has to do that. He knocks on her door and though she doesn't ask him to enter, he does. He sits on the chair next to her bed and he sees she's not in the mood for a chat, yet, he doesn't cease himself from confronting her.

'Where were you last night? I know you slept away from home.' He says with a stern look.

'Why the hell will you want to know where I spent the night?'

'Why are you are so pissed? Someone fucked you, right?' He asks irritatingly.

'Of course! I was fucked and he did it really well.'

'Wow, great.' He says, 'So you think you'd like daddy knowing about this?'

'Fuck daddy!' She yells at him, 'You think I don't know what the hell transpired between you and Vera?'

Completely shocked to hear this from her, his heart thumps suddenly like never before and his jaw drops open instantly.

'She told you?'

'Just shut up! Shut up and get the hell out of my room before I shout it into everyone's ear!'

He shuts up, gets up, and walks out quietly. He leaves straightway to the basketball court. He doesn't meet a full house there because it's a Sunday morning and many of the local folks were off to church.

He only meets a couple of sucky players practicing to improve their poor skills and a couple of lovebirds utilizing the empty seats to their advantage. However, he doesn't feel like returning home at that instant. He knows Vera is really mad at him and has been avoiding him ever since the incident but he just didn't expect that she would tell his junior sister about it.

He feels like he has his hand in the mouth of a shark now and definitely has to do something to get them out. He begins to plot a trap against Vera which he thinks should effectively silence her over the issue, and only hopes that Vera hadn't told his dad already.

The couple return home at 12pm when Nicholas is still away and Vanessa hasn't come out of her room since breakfast. They climb upstairs and decide to see Vanessa before they enter their bedroom but she declines to see them. Thirty minutes later, Anita serves Vanessa lunch in her bedroom because she has refused to dine with them. Just as Anita is heading out of the room, Vanessa asks her to lock the door and return. She does just as she asks and sits by her on the bed.

With a stern look on her face, Vanessa asks her to tell her how well he fucked her and whether she enjoyed it. She pretends not to understand what Vanessa is saying but she repeats herself and this time, more elaborately.

'You've been sleeping with my brother. How well does he fuck you? Huh!'

'No, never… Please, no' She denies vehemently.

'O, I see. You are denying, right? Say no again and I'll let everyone hear about it.'

She falls on her knees instantly and pleads tearfully, 'No, please… Don't. He seduced me and I couldn't hold myself up. I swear I was a virgin and didn't want him to. Ever since, he's been manipulating me at every opportunity.'

'Really? So, it's not just once? So, you think you love him?'

She nods her head and says, 'I've not been able to take him out of my mind since he deflowered me.'

'Well, I'm sorry girl' Vanessa says emotionlessly, 'men have no heart and my brother… he's the worst of their kind. He just used you. To him, you are just a lady that made herself available and he will screw anyone who presents herself, even your big sister.

Those words break Anita's heart completely and she begins to weep but Vanessa says to her, 'Please don't weep here. You can do that in the next room, where you enjoyed moaning irritatingly to my hearing.'

Anita gets up and walks slowly towards the door. She unlocks it and walks out but Mr. McFall who is on his way to fetch something from his room sees her coming from Vanessa's room. He begins walking towards her and she quickly dries her tears. He asks if everything is okay and she says yes. He carries on and makes it into Vanessa's room, sits by her and pleads with her to be nice to the workers despite the gap in their social status.

She nods to everything he says and points her right forefinger towards the door right after he's done speaking. He notices she's definitely nowhere near being in a chatty mood.

However, before he walks out, he informs her that due to reasons beyond his control, he will have to be away again during the coming weekdays.

After eating supper in her room and some minutes past 7pm, Vanessa finally walks out of her room to go see Peter. As she descends and nears the hall, she sees her dad and stepmom kissing in the couch at the hall. She feels a sudden stream of rage gushing through her veins and wishes she could just go there and smash Vera's head with a beer bottle. However, she manages to cool herself down and walks briskly past them. Her dad calls her name but he walks out on him.

Upon reaching Peter's cabin, she notices the door isn't locked and she enters in. She enters Peter's bedroom stealthily and hears him singing in the bath. Minutes later, he comes out of the bathroom wearing just a pant and his towel lying over his shoulders. He's startled upon seeing Vanessa; he quickly raps the towel around his waist and then takes a seat beside her on the bed.

Just as he's about to say a word to her, she shushes him by placing her forefinger on his mouth and says, 'No words, just fuck me.'

She begins to strip off; he shuts his eyes, opens them a minute later and sees her lying completely naked on his bed. He is a bit reluctant to touch but can't get himself to stop stealing glances at her sexy naked body. Finally, he takes off the towel, pulls his pant down, and lies beside her on the bed.

Vanessa holds his dick – it's her first time ever – and begins to pull on it. He squeezes her firm young breasts and then begin to suck on them incessantly and she begins to moan undertone. She guides his hands towards her vagina and he begins to rub firmly on her clitoris. She screams instantly and her thighs shut involuntarily but he parts them open again and rubs on them some more.

After a while, as she's already thinking she's being overwhelmingly satisfied, he sticks his mouth into her vagina and begins to eat it out. She struggles to contain the sexual ecstasy; her veins draw up around her neck, and she pushes his head away.

She screams loudly as her body experiences a spasm orgasm; her pussy squirts and her body squirms uncontrollably.

After a while, he holds her down and sticks his dick into her tight pussy. She screams painfully after the first thrust, wearing an ambivalent look on her face as her deflowered pussy emanates virgin blood.

He takes a tissue paper, wipes the blood, and continues to penetrate her slowly and enjoyably.

Vanessa returns home at 11pm feeling so excited and accomplished. As she enters her bathhouse to pass urine, she hears a lady moaning pleasurably from Nicholas' room again; but whether it is Emily or Anita or her stepmom, she thinks she doesn't care anymore. She's just so overjoyed with how sweetly she has been deflowered.

CHAPTER 8

It's Monday morning. Mr. McFall had left around 6am and Nicholas' plan to avoid meeting his father until he left has been successfully executed. Nicholas leaves his room, descends and begins to walk outside. Vera manages to speak to him for the first time in a week and it's because Stevie had told her to do so with the kids.

She asks him where he is headed and he tells her with a broad smile on her face that he's going to buy some stuffs from town. Vera is irritated because she thinks, after having seen her full glare nakedness, that smile on his face is meant to mock her.

However, she hides the ugly feeling and decides not to talk about it all.

He doesn't return until 2pm, by which time Vanessa had already left the house. On his way upstairs, he meets Juan on the stairs. She tells him Vera has sent her to get some wine from the kitchen. Nicholas perceives it's a perfect opportunity to execute the wicked plan he had conjured a day ago.

He knows Vera and Juan have become fond of each other; they chat a lot and sometimes share a drink or even dine together. He follows Juan and engages her in a chat to the kitchen. Juan fills a serving tray with a bottle of wine and two wineglasses containing ice cubes but then, Nicholas sends her on an errand to go fetch Anita for him before she takes the stuff to Vera.

Just as she leaves the kitchen, he pulls out a sachet of Spanish fly from his pocket; he had bought it from town that day. He pours some drops into the wineglasses and shakes them until they're evenly matched with the ice cubes.

Juan returns right after he is done, picks them up and takes them away unsuspectingly. Meanwhile, he leads Anita to his room and hands over a bunch of dirty clothing to her to do the laundry. She carries them downstairs albeit feeling sad that Nicholas didn't exhibit any romantic signs towards her.

He walks out of his room and into the hallway, stands behind the window to Vera's bedroom, and pries on their conversation. He finds a small space around the curtains and he peeps into the room. He sees them seated excitedly by each other on the bed with a magazine in hand, and Vera in a skimpy skirt and soft blouse as usual.

They drink the wine and as the minutes pass, their electrifying mood begins to dwindle gradually and their voices begin to sound feebler and more emotional. After about five minutes, Vera asks Juan to give her a massage. Vera lies down on her belly; Juan sits on the back of her thighs and begins to massage her back.

With their heads facing the direction opposite to the entrance, Nicholas opens the door gently and walks stealthily into the room for a better a visual. He gets himself a corner where he's able to hide himself comfortably; yet, getting a good visual of them.

Juan keeps on massaging, taking occasional sips from the wine, and their libidos keep surging until they reach unbearable levels. Juan migrates her palms from Vera's shoulders to her buttocks. She caresses them; Vera begins to moan pleasurably, turns herself about and with a bittersweet look on her face, she tells Juan to stop but she just doesn't.

Juan slots her palms into her bra, pulls her breasts out and squeezes her nipples. Vera, at that point, is so already so wet. Juan sticks her fingers into Vera's vagina, works out her clitoris and that takes her to the point of no return.

They strip their clothing off, Juan puts her head between Vera's thighs and eats her pussy delightfully. Vera tries to contain the unbearable pleasure but struggles to keep her moans undertone.

Meanwhile Vanessa, who has just returned home after another fantastic sexual bout with Peter, climbs upstairs and a few steps into the hallway, she hears some sexual moans emanating from one of the rooms. She notices it's coming from her parent's bedroom but she knows her dad is supposed to be gone. She figures out it's Nicholas and her stepmom at it again. She walks furiously towards the room, finds the door lying ajar and she enters in but Juan continues to eat out her pussy because they don't hear nor see her enter. As Vanessa walks closer, she notices it's not Nicholas but a lady.

'What the fuck!' She shrieks.

Vera raises her head immediately and upon seeing Vanessa, she pushes Juan's head out of her thighs. Vera quickly wraps herself in a bedspread and chases after Vanessa who is speeding into her room.

Meanwhile Juan, skipping to wear her undergarments, slips into her dress in a lightning speed and races downstairs. Nicholas who had been spying on them with a firm strong erection – seeing nobody caught him – springs out of his hiding place and hurries downstairs after Juan.

He enters Juan's room and finds her sitting on the bed. She is terrified upon seeing him and says, 'Please, I'm really sorry… forgive me. I don't know what came over me.'

He sits by her on the bed, shushes her, and says, 'It's alright. Stuff like this happen. You were just acting on your sexual emotions.'

She tries to speak again but he halts her and says, 'Right now, with my sister finding out about you guys, I'm the only one that can convince my dad that it never happened. I know you are still feeling horny right now, aren't you?'

She nods guiltily; he touches her thighs but she pushes his hands away and says tearfully, 'What are you doing? I'm already in trouble.'

'And I am the solution. I'll defend both of you and deny it happened. Besides, I'm just helping satisfy to you right now. I can smell your wet craving pussy.'

She turns away and says frustratingly, 'Do you even realize I'm five years older than you are?'

Nicholas ignores her statement and pushes her onto the bed; parts her thighs and, against her wishes, performs cunnilingus on her. She is very nervous but Nicholas persistently eats out her pussy till she's engulfed in pleasure. He makes her kneel on the bed, bends her over, inserts his dick into her extremely wet pussy and fucks her from behind. She's unable to keep her sexual moans undertone and that draws the attention of Anita who is washing just a few meters away from the window. She draws closer, peeps and is absolutely stunned to see Nicholas fucking her sister.

'You bustard! Fuck you! fuck you!' Anita exclaims furiously and runs indoors, cursing Nicholas all the way to the door but she's unable to enter because it's locked.

CHAPTER 9

After incessant pleas and tears by Vera, Vanessa has her mind made-up. She calls her dad and informs him of all the happenings.

He is totally shocked, disappointed and infuriated so much by the news that he orders the security to ensure no one left the house until he arrived. He arrives five hours later after taking an emergency flight back.

At the time, he does, Nicholas is still locked up in Juan's room because Anita is standing behind the door with a knife, threatening to kill him and everyone around was scared to get close. Meanwhile, Vanessa is seated with the chef and gardener at the hall whiles Vera – feeling totally guilty and degraded – has locked herself up in the bedroom. Anita, still very furious, accords Stevie the much needed respect when he approaches her and hands the knife over to him.

He takes Nicholas and Vanessa upstairs whiles entreating the rest of them to stay calm downstairs. He knocks severally and continually on the door that Vera lets them in but she refuses to. After having spent about five minutes standing behind the door, Stevie breaks into room. They find her lying on the floor unconscious after having deliberately overdosed on some drugs.

Stevie carries her up with the help of the others, rushes her into his car and drives her hastily to the hospital.

The medics attend to her immediately; they tell them she's in a very critical state and might not survive for long but they would do their possible best to resuscitate her. Stevie and his kids return from the doctor's office and take their seats in the treatment room. Stevie is so broken and scared of losing her.

He weeps as he beholds her laying down unconsciously and Vanessa, beginning to feel repentant, consoles him. He calls Nicholas to sit by him too and, still sobbing, begins to tell the real story of their mom:

"I really loved your mom and would have done anything for her. But one day, while Vera and I had to come home impromptu for some documents, we caught her making out with her own cousin in the hall.

I was so brokenhearted and disgusted that I wanted to divorce her but Vera advised that for the sake of my kids, I overlooked a divorce which I did. I could never touch her again; she couldn't look into my face anymore out of guiltiness and she took to drinking which resulted in her death in the car crash.

Vera was my only confidant who always encouraged me and strengthened me emotionally, even before she died and after her death, Vera was the only one satisfying my emotional needs. I craved for more than that and one day, I attempted to make out with her but she resisted.

She was a virgin but I was horny so after many failed attempts to seduce her, I raped her. I feared she would report to the police but she didn't. She just quit the job and avoided me for over a month. When I finally found her, she was one month pregnant and I had to really beg her to marry me before she agreed.

Unfortunately, she had a miscarriage. Not wanting you guys to live with bitter memories of your mom, we agreed never to tell you the truth."

The revelation strikes Nicholas and Vanessa to the core of their hearts. Nicholas tearfully confesses the whole truth of the lesbian saga and his attempted rape on her. Vera regains consciousness some hours later but passes away in less than ten minutes.

A week after, they perform her burial ceremony in Dallas. Vanessa and her dad relocate permanently to their old mansion in Dallas; Peter and Yvonne come along with them and Stevie sponsors their education. However, Nicholas travels far away from his home; shackled in the burden of guilt which he's never able to take off his shoulders and cuts all ties.

I write under the pseudonym: Urquhart Randolph. I like to write great romance stories that take you on a blazing journey - tears, laughter (may be both) or just a steamy hot fun (perhaps all of them).

Please... leave a review, regardless if you think my book deserves 1* or 5 * let me know if you had enjoyed this great story?

THANK YOU ☺

VISIT US
WWW.GLOFTON.COM
Enroll in our VIP list.
Be the first to be notified on our latest published book.
Downloading for free gifts.

www.ingramcontent.com/pod-product-compliance
Lightning Source LLC
Chambersburg PA
CBHW071350130626
46556CB00005B/2120